the Deepest Breath

Meg Grehan

Houghton Mifflin Harcourt
Boston   New York

hmhbooks.com

First published in Ireland as *The Deepest Breath*, by Little Island Books, 2019

The text was set in Centaur MT Std.
Hand-lettering by Andrea Miller
Interior design by Andrea Miller

Library of Congress Cataloging-in-Publication Data
Names: Grehan, Meg, author.
Title: Deepest breath / Meg Grehan.
Description: Boston : Houghton Mifflin Harcourt, 2021. | Originally
published in Dublin, Ireland, by Little Island Books in 2019. |
Audience: Ages 10 to 12. | Audience: Grades 4–6. | Summary: Struggling
with her feelings for a female classmate, an eleven-year-old Irish girl
tries to confide in her mother, the person she trusts most in the world.
Identifiers: LCCN 2019037075 (print) | LCCN 2019037076 (ebook) | ISBN
9780358354758 (hardcover) | ISBN 9780358355458 (ebook)
Subjects: CYAC: Novels in verse. | Identity—Fiction. |
Self-acceptance—Fiction. | Coming out (Sexual orientation)—Fiction. |
Lesbians—Fiction. | Mothers and daughters—Fiction.
Classification: LCC PZ7.5.G7 De 2021 (print) | LCC PZ7.5.G7 (ebook) | DDC
[Fic]—dc23
LC record available at https://lccn.loc.gov/2019037075
LC ebook record available at https://lccn.loc.gov/2019037076

Manufactured in the United States of America
DOC 10 9 8 7 6 5 4 3 2 1
4500815514

For Dylan
For always making everything
A little less scary

I know a lot of things
About a lot of things
But the thing I know the most about
Is me
Stevie

I know that I am eleven years and two months old
And that my hair is brown
And my eyes are green
And I'm allergic to peanuts

I know I have a mum
Whose room is right next to mine
And that sometimes we tap and scratch on the wall at night
Morse code is good for scaring nightmares away
I know that

I know I have a dad
And I know that he lives far away
And I know that's not my fault
And I know that that's
OK

I know that I have a funny name
Because the doctors said my mum was going to have a baby
    boy
But then I popped out
A slimy wriggly baby girl
And she liked the name too much by then
So Stevie it was
And Stevie I am

I know I like the color purple
And things that sparkle
And science and books
And cats and stars and space

I know that I broke my pinkie finger once
And that now
It sticks out funny

I know I'm afraid of zombies and clowns
And not much else
I know I can be brave
But that sometimes it's hard

I know a lot
About me

There's only one thing
In the whole of me
That I don't know

It's something funny
It's in my chest
And sometimes my tummy
And always my head
It's a fizzy feeling
Warm and squishy
And it makes me blush
And it only happens
When I look at my friend
Chloe

And I don't know what it is
Exactly

two

At school I share a desk
With Chloe
And Andrew
And Robert
Us girls on one side
And the boys on the other

Robert likes football
And is really good at math
Way better than me

And he's nice
Though we don't talk much
Mostly he talks to Andrew

Andrew has been my friend
Ever since we were babies
And even though we didn't choose to be friends
I'm glad we are
Though we don't talk at school too much
Because I read a lot
And he likes to listen to Robert
Talk about football
Way more than I thought anyone could

Chloe paints her nails
A new color
Every week

On Mondays they are sleek and shiny and new
And on Fridays
They are all

Chipped
And bitten
And you have to look
Really close
To see what color they were

But I always know what color they were

I know last week they were pink
And the week before they were yellow
And the week before that they were orange
With tiny black bats on her pinkie nails
For Halloween

Chloe bites her nails
And the last of her nail polish
(Green this week, with sparkles)
Falls like radioactive snow onto our desk

I wipe some off my book
And try to concentrate

We're learning about
Whales

Whales scare me a little
Because they're so big
That I must be
So small
But still
I try to concentrate
And I write down
The most interesting things
In my notebook

My notebook
Is gigantic
It has five hundred pages
And a yellow cover
And a ribbon
For keeping your place
I've only used 124 pages
So far

But I will use them all
I'll fill them up
And when every page
Is full of words

I'll know
Just about
Everything
There is
To know

After school my auntie Judith picks me up
Because Mum is still at work
And it's way too cold to walk
Although honestly
I think I could handle it
Because I've read about explorers
Who've survived way worse
And it isn't even snowing

But Mum says I'll catch my death
Which sounds
Dramatic
And scary
So I buckle myself into Auntie Judith's car
And I listen as she tells me about
"The absolute rubbish the boss came out with today"

At dinner I tell Mum about whales

"And then there's the bowhead whale
And no one really knows how long they live
But once
Scientists found one
With a weapon from 1879
Eighteen seventy-nine!
Embedded in it
And that means
That it might've been
More than one hundred years old!
A hundred!
And once
They examined a bowhead whale's eyes
And the amino acid inside them
Means that one of them
Might've lived to 211
Two hundred and eleven!"

And she gasps
And I feel smart
And interesting
And good good good
Except for deep inside
Where I feel

A squirming kind of
Fear

I have a nightmare that night
The first in three years
And seven months

I dream about the sea
Deep down
Where it isn't really blue
But black
Like bruises or ink or midnight
Where you can't tell up from down
Or right from left
Where there's nowhere to go

I wake and I'm still underwater
And for a second
I hold my breath
Even though it hurts

Even though it feels like there's gallons and gallons and
    gallons of water
Pressing down on my chest
Pinning me to my bed
I fling my arm out
Searching for the switch
To turn
My lamp
On to fill
The room
With light and then
When it's on
When the room
Is orange
And warm
I can breathe
And the water is gone

I sit up in bed for the rest of the night
And read a book
I run my fingers across every page
Under every line
Every word
I make myself focus

On the paper
On how
Dry it is
And that
Makes me feel
Safe

I don't like my room to be
Messy
But I think it likes to be
Just a little
Because it always is

I think it must do it
All by itself
Maybe while I'm asleep
Or at school
Or reading
Or whenever I look away
For just a minute

Because my clothes are always
On the floor
And I swear

I didn't put them there
On purpose

And because my teddies
Don't like to stay on my bed
In their neat line
When they have places to be
And important business to discuss

And because books never seem to make it
Back to their shelves at night
They have sleepovers under my bed
And holidays on my desk
And naps under my pillow

But I think
That's OK
Because maybe
When I sleep
They'll whisper to me
And maybe
When I wake up
Everything might make
Just a little
More sense

By the time the sun comes up
I've decided
I won't tell Mum about the nightmare
I've decided
I don't want to worry her

My mum worries a lot
About a lot of things
I don't think she knows that I know
But I see it
I see how she picks at her nail beds
And looks all around her
When a what-if pops into her head
And I
Definitely
Don't want to be a
What-if

three

Chloe's nails are blue today
And she's talking about magic

Chloe is great at magic
Which makes sense to me
Though I'm not sure why

She can flip cards and make little balls disappear
And she can pull coins from behind your ear

I know it isn't real
I do

But there's a part of me that doesn't
At the same time

It's raining
So hard you can barely hear anything else
And at lunch
We have to stay inside

I try to read my book but the noise of the rain
And my whole class yelling
All at once
Makes my head
Feel like it might fall off
So instead
I watch Chloe practice her magic

"For my next trick!"
Chloe says
In a voice that sounds like
Glitter and cotton candy and popping candy
"I'll need
A lovely assistant!"

I stare at her hands
At her blue nail polish
And the way she's holding the playing cards
Like she knows
Knows for certain
That she won't drop them
Even though there's so many
And I know
For sure
I would drop them

"Stevie

       Stevie?"

I blink
And she's looking at me

"That's you"
She says

"What's me?"
I say

"My lovely assistant"
She says

And I say
Nothing
Instead my throat closes a little
And chomps down whatever words I would've said

Her lovely assistant

"OK"
I say
And my voice sounds funny
Not at all like my voice
More like
A squeak

"Pick a card
Any card!"
She booms

And I do
I pick a
Three of hearts
And blush a little

Why am I blushing?

And put it back in the pack

                                        I don't know

She shuffles the cards
In a showy
Exaggerated way
And it looks so cool
I can't take my eyes off her hands
Then

"Ta-da!
Is this your card?"
She booms
Not caring that she's louder than everyone else in the room
    combined
Or that she's made Andrew and Robert both jump
I laugh a little
Because they look so startled
But also
Because
It is my card
And despite all the things I know
I have no idea
How she's done it
And for once

For the first time
I love not knowing

four

I know a lot of things
I know that
Because I can look at my notebook
And see pages and pages of things I know
And because people say it
A lot
Sometimes in a good way
Sometimes not

But there are so many things
That I don't know
There are so many things to know
And the list gets bigger every single day

New plants are found
New animals are discovered
Inventions invented
Diseases diagnosed
Places charted
Words spoken
Decisions made

And sometimes
It all feels
Too much
Too big

Like I'm running behind a train
And it's chugging along
Fast fast faster
And I'll never catch up

I don't even know everything
There is to know
About trains

It makes my stomach ache

Thinking about it

It makes my stomach ache
And my head feel
Noisy

I tell my mum at dinner
When she's putting too much cheese on her spaghetti
                                     Mountains of cheese
I tell her
I feel like everything moves too much
And I feel
Like everything is too much
And I'll never understand it all
Or know it all
Or see it all
And it makes me
Sad
And angry
And tired
And over-over-overwhelmed

Mum stops piling grated cheese on her food
And looks at me
Like she isn't sure what to say

This happens sometimes
And I always
Always feel bad
Because she worries

I can see the worry
Slip into her head
And pour down her face

Her eyes get darker
And her smile changes

I don't want her to worry
I don't

"Why do you think you feel that way?
Like you need to know
Everything?"
Mum asks
Like she really wants to know

Like she really wants to
Understand

So I tell her
I tell her how I feel like
Knowing things
Makes me safe
Makes me powerful
Makes me
In control

How I think of bad things
Sometimes
Things that might happen
Things that could happen

They pop into my head
With no warning
With no
Permission
And they play like movies
Like horrible movies
Horror movies
Movies she would never let me see
If she could stop it

But she can't
And I can't

I tell her
How I need to know
Just in case
Bad things happen
Small bad things
Or big bad things
Or in-between bad things

Because what if a Bad Thing happens
And I don't know the thing
The One Thing
That could stop it
And I don't know that thing
What then

Mum takes a bite of pasta
And makes a "Hmm" sound
And she looks
Thoughtful

This is one of the things
I love love love about my mum

She thinks about every answer
She thinks hard
And when she gives me answers
I always know
They're real and true answers

So I eat my dinner
And I wait

"OK"
Mum says
And she tells me
That no one knows everything
And that that's OK
And I nod along

She tells me
That bad things might happen
But that bad things
Might *not* happen
Too

She tells me that when a Bad Thing
Pops into my head
I should tell her
So she can help me figure it out
And that if I can't tell her right away
That I should
Write it down
On a piece of paper
And I should fold the paper up
And leave the Bad Thing there
In the ink
On the paper
Until we can deal with it
Together

Then
She says
"Why not make a list
A list of the things
You most want to know
And start with those"

And
I say

"That's a great idea"

So we do it
We eat spaghetti then we bundle ourselves up
And we go for a walk
And we puff out our breath like dragons
And we look for constellations
And we make a list

The Things I Want to Know About the Most:

1. The ocean and all the things that live there and
   why it's so scary
2. The stars and all the constellations
3. How phones work
4. What happened to Princess Anastasia
5. Knots

When we've come home from our walk
And Mum's washed the dishes

And I've finished my homework
Mum tucks me in
And kisses me on the head
And turns on my reading light
And goes

But instead of reading
I get my list
My Things I Want to Know About list
And add
One more thing
One extra-important thing
The thing I most need to know

6. What is the fizzy feeling in my chest

five

I have a dream about my dad
Which isn't weird
Because it happens
Every few months
Like my brain just needs to
Check in
Every now
And then

I dream that he's sitting in our garden
On the grass

And there's frost on his fingers
And his eyelashes
And his shoelaces
But he doesn't look
Cold
He doesn't
Shiver
Or shake
He just sits
Looking
Up up up
At the sky
And when I open my mouth
To say hi
He puts a sparkling finger to his lips
So I look up too
And I see
The stars
And they're close
They're closer than ever
Big and white and shining bright bright bright
And I can hear them
Talking to each other
Tiny voices
Like they haven't noticed us
Like they're much too

Busy

Much too

Important

For us tiny little things

With our funny little bodies

Our cold noses

Our goosebumps

Our breath erupting

Like tiny clouds

Proving we're here and alive and real

And that thought

Is so strangely

Comforting

That I sit down

Beside my dad

On the cold grass

And we just

Watch

And listen

And the stars

Float down

So slowly

We hardly even notice

Until they're around us

And we can't even tell

If they're on the ground

Or we're in the sky
And either way
Is fine by us

When I wake up
I write it all down
The stars and the frost and the magic of it all
I write it all
Fast as I can
In case it escapes my head
So fast that I spell words wrong
And my handwriting is scratchy and messy
And it doesn't matter
Because all that matters
Is not forgetting

We used to go for walks
Dad and me
Always late at night
Only on nights
With stars
He'd wake me up

With a little
Shake
And a happy
"They're bright tonight!"
Then he'd wrap me in wool
Until I waddled
Coat, scarf, hat, mittens
Check, check, check, check
We'd take his big flashlight
I'd hold it
With both hands
Until my arms ached
And I'd wait
For fear to twist in my belly
For shadows to move
And trees to creak
For a beast to appear in the flashlight
But we'd just walk
All alone in the quiet
And he'd point out
Constellations
He'd tell me their names
And what they meant
And I always wondered
How he knew
Because he didn't read books

Or talk about
Smart stuff
But asking
Felt mean
And I
Felt mean
For thinking it
But he didn't know
He just pointed at stars
And on those nights
He was the smartest
And when the flashlight
Became too heavy
He'd take it
And my hand
In his big scratchy hands
And we'd go home

I miss him sometimes
And I used to feel guilty
For not missing him
All the time
But now I think that's OK

Because I have all I need here
And hopefully he has all he needs there

At breakfast I write the dream out
Neat and proper
On a nice fresh sheet of paper
And Mum finds me an envelope
(A pink one that's really for a birthday card but Dad won't
    mind)
And we write his address on the front
And I lick the stamp
And then we walk to the post box
And she tells me about her dreams

Six

Mum gets me a book

She gives it to me the next day after school

And says it's an early Christmas present

Because I'm so good

Which makes me blush

And she says she hopes it will help me

Tick one thing off the list

Which makes me excited

It's a massive book

Gigantic and heavy and full of big words and colorful
photos

The Ocean and Its Inhabitants

I flick through
And fear makes my spine feel wobbly
Like I might crumple
But I want to know
I want to understand
Everything there is to know
Everything there is to understand
So I flick to page one
And I open my notebook
And I start reading

First
I read about the
Cookie-cutter shark
A small shark
That eats by cutting circles out of fish bellies
With its sharp little teeth

Every single day
They swim up
Up up up
To the top
So they break the surface
At dusk

And at dawn
They turn
And they go back
Down down down
Into the sea
Only to turn back around
Again

I don't know why they do that
Not yet
But I think
That's kind of how I feel
About learning things
Like I read and read and I get to the top of the pile
But by the time the sun comes back up
There's so much more to know
And I need to start again
And I'm anxious again

At school the next day
I'm tired
I'm tired through and through
Because dreams keep coming
Sometimes dreams

Sometimes nightmares
Sometimes something in the middle
Always vivid and long and way
Way too
Real

Even the good ones
Feel too big for my brain
I wake sleepy
As if my body slept
But my brain
Worked and worked
All night
And in the morning
It has nothing left over

In the morning we have a spelling test
Then we do math
And then it's lunchtime

I don't like lunchtime
Especially in winter
It's cold and loud and boring

I sit on the best bench
Beside the best tree
And I read
A book about a boy
With an alien for a brother
And a best friend named
Sarah

I think the boy has a crush on Sarah
Because he blushes when he talks to her sometimes
And he wants to hold her hand
But I'm not sure
Because I don't blush when I talk to Andrew
And I definitely don't want to hold his hand
So maybe
I really don't know what a crush is

Sometimes Mum says I'm going to marry Andrew
Because I've known him since we were babies
And we've always been best friends
But she always says it
With a smile
And a little laugh

So I'm not really sure
If it's a truth or a joke

If it is a truth
I don't feel very happy about it
And if it is a joke
I don't think it's a very good one

But I don't want to hurt
Mum's feelings
So I laugh
A small not-real laugh
It's not a lie
It's just a little empty
Is all

I don't want to marry Andrew
That's one of the things I know
Andrew is nice
And we still get along
Pretty well
Even though he likes football a lot now
And I don't
He's still nice to me

And I'm still nice to him
I like when he comes over
And when we watch movies
And bake
I know that I think he's interesting
And that I'm glad I know him
But I know
For sure
I don't want to marry him
And I wish
My mum wouldn't say it
Because it makes me worry
That maybe
She means it
That maybe
That's what she sees when she pictures me grown-up
And I don't think
That's what my grown-up self
Will be

When I'm just about to finish page 164
Something happens
Something bad
I know it's bad because it's loud and fast

And everyone gasps
And then there's a split second
Of silence
And then a wail

I look up and
Chloe
Is on the ground
And she's clutching her knee
And I see red
Sneaking through her gray tights
And I hear someone yell
"Find Ms. Matthews!"
And before I know it
I'm up
I'm off the bench
And I'm running
Running running
All the way over
To Chloe
Which is funny
Because I don't remember telling my legs to move
But they do it anyway
And I don't tell them to stop

Chloe is crying so hard
Her face is all red
And she has snot dripping down to her lips
And she looks
So sad
It makes my heart hurt
In a sudden
Spiky way

So I take her hand
And my lips start to say
"It's OK, Chloe!"
Over and over
And I pull her up off the ground
And I say I'll take her to the nurse
And she holds my hand
Really really hard
But that's OK
And we hobble inside
Her limping
And me pretending my hand isn't being crushed

When we get to the nurse
Chloe is still crying

But a little less
Which is a relief
Because then my hand
And my heart
Hurt a little less
But then something strange happens
And I don't know what it means
Chloe
Lets go of my hand
And suddenly
I feel
Sad
Sad in the pit of my tummy
Sad to the tips of my fingers
And I think
I want her to keep holding my hand
And I wonder
Why

Chloe hugs me then
A bear hug
Big and welcoming and warm
She wraps me up

Somehow
Even though we're the same size
She wraps me up and squeezes tight
And whispers
"Thanks, Stevie"
And then my hand doesn't hurt anymore
Not at all

The nurse cleans Chloe's knee
And slathers on a cream
That even smells sting-y
And Chloe cries a bit
And squeezes my hand again
Then the nurse puts a bright orange bandage over the cut
And tells Chloe she was very brave
And me that I was very kind

Afterwards
Back in the hallway on the way to class
Chloe says
"Thank you"

In a quiet
Extra-nice way
And I say
"No problem"
And I make sure
Not to look up
To keep staring down at the ground
Counting tiles
Just in case
She sees my bright pink cheeks

At home that night
I tell Mum all about it
Even about how
My heart felt light and heavy
And real and not real
And fast and slow
All at the same time
And she says
Maybe
I should be a doctor when I grow up
Or a firefighter
But I really don't think that
That's what my heart was trying to tell me

My mum
Loves me
So much

I know it as much as I feel it
Which is
Lots and lots
And for sure

I have exactly 42 pages left
Of my book
About fish
And then
Surely
After 274 whole pages
I'll know all
There is
To know

The Sea section of my notebook is the longest yet
It takes up pages and pages and pages
Because the sea is big

So the list of things to know
Is just as big
But I'm almost there

I know that bull sharks
Are the crankiest type of shark
That they're territorial
And they'll snap if you barge into their space
Which I think is understandable
And that they don't like
Bright colors
At all
And my mum says
They're the teenagers of the sea
And I'm not sure what exactly she means by that
But she made herself laugh when she said it
So that's good

I know that the *Spirobranchus giganteus*
Is also called the
Christmas tree worm

Because that's what it looks like
A little Christmas tree
All bright and small and cute
Tiny colorful fir forests
Decorating coral reefs

I know that sea angels
Are actually called
Cliones
And that they're called angels
Because they're translucent
And kind of cute
And ethereal
And they float around
Like
Tiny little angels
Though I would've called them
Sea ghosts
Because that's what they look like
To me
Spooky and lonely

I know that the fin whale
Is the second biggest
After the blue whale
And that they're longer
And thinner
Like big chunky eels
I watched a video of one
Leaping up out of the water
Its whole gigantic body streaming out
Long and lanky and beautiful in a scary way
It gave me nightmares
But I watched it again the next day anyway

I know that octopuses

          (Not octopi
          I know that too)

Have three hearts
Two of them pump blood

          (Which is blue
          Another thing I know!)

To their gills
And the third heart
Pumps blood to all the other organs

I know that that one stops working when the octopus
    swims
Which is why they like to crawl around
With their eight tentacles
Which, I know,
Each has a brain of its own
One big brain in the octopus's head
And eight smaller ones in each tentacle
Nine brains!
Imagine how much you could know with nine brains
I like octopuses
I think if I were an animal
I'd like to be an octopus
Even though the sea is scary
I think all that fear
Might be worth it
For three hearts
Nine brains
And blue blood

Andrew comes over after school
Sometimes
When his dad has work

We watch movies
Or we play games on the computer
But today
We bake cookies

Andrew is great at baking
Especially cookies
He barely even needs to look at the recipe
Even though he keeps his recipe book in his backpack
It's a notebook
Smaller than mine
And bright red
And it used to be shiny
But now it's covered in stickers
It has sticky notes and magazine cuttings poking out
And shiny paper clips holding everything together

It looks cool
It looks
Like it belongs to Andrew
Like even if a stranger found it
They would know
It was Andrew's
Because it couldn't possibly belong to anyone else

He never lets me look inside
Because he says his recipes are
Top Secret
And will make him
Super Famous
Someday
And I'm pretty sure
He's right

My job is finding things
Eggs, flour, butter, sugar, chocolate chips
So Andrew can do
Whatever it is he does

He looks happy when he bakes
He laughs more
Even at my worst jokes
And he smiles the whole time
Except for when he focuses
Really hard
And then his tongue pokes out
He looks funny
In the most brilliant way

When Andrew slides the tray into the oven
And sets our pink piggy-shaped oven timer
For 20 minutes
I decide
That I'm going to ask him

I ask Andrew
Because just like me
Andrew knows a lot of things
But Andrew
Knows things
That I don't
Andrew knows things
That I never even thought to know

He knows how much sugar goes into cookies
And how to make even the tallest cake stand up straight
He knows what sodium bicarbonate does
How to make icing
And what gluten is

"Hey
Andy
You know
Chloe"

My voice sounds scratchy
And higher than usual
Like it's had to squeeze every word out of me

"Chloe who sits with us?
Magic Chloe?"

Magic Chloe
I like that
I file it away
In the back of my head

"Yeah
What do you
Think about
Her?
Like
Do you
Like her?"

"Like her?
Or like her like her?"

Oh
Oh

I'm not sure what to say
So I settle for

"Either
I guess"

He plops down on the floor
Cross-legged in front of the oven
His nose nearly pressed up against the glass of the door
Andrew is very protective of his cookies

"I like her"
He says
Eventually
"She's nice
And she's good at magic
I still don't know how she does the thing with the balls
You know when there's three then —"

"Then five
I can't figure it out either!"

We smile at each other
Real smiles
But there's a worry in my chest
A Worry
That Andrew likes Chloe
Likes her likes her
And if he likes her
Then maybe she likes him
Likes him likes him
And that idea
That Idea
Makes me
Sad
Immeasurably sad
Painfully sad

"But"
He says then
"I don't think
I like her
More than that
I don't think so"

And he stares at the cookies
The hot orange glow on his face
Makes his eyes
Sparkle a bit
And it looks
In that moment
It looks like he has
Just as many thoughts
Just as many
Questions
As I do
And I don't know
If I feel better
Or worse

"Do you like
I mean
Like
Anyone?"

I don't look at him when I ask
I couldn't
Even if I really really wanted to
But when I do peek up

He isn't looking at me
Either

"I don't know"
He says it so quietly I almost miss it
"Maybe"

And then the timer goes off
And we look at each other
In a way I think only
Friends
Can
A way that means
"I don't know either
But I'm with you"

And I say
"I didn't think it would be so hard to tell"
And he says
"Me neither"
Soft and sad
And we take out the cookies
And they're perfect
As always

Chloe is definitely my friend now
I think she was before
But I know she is now
She runs up to me in the morning
All smiles and questions
"How are you?
Did you do the math homework?
Did you think number three was impossible because I sure
    did?
Do you like magic?
Have you read the new Wizards of Westerly Station book?
Who was your favorite?
Did you cry when Steph died?
Do you have any brothers?
Or sisters?
What do your parents do?
Does she like it?
Where's your dad?
Do you miss him?
What did you have for breakfast?"

I've never talked this much
To anyone
Maybe Mum
But definitely
No one else

But I answer all her questions
And I don't even mind

"I'm good
Yes, I did
Number three was hard but I got it in the end
Magic is cool, I guess
I'm only on book three of Wizards
Steph was my favorite until
Yeah, I cried when she died
No
No
My mum works in an office
I think she likes it
A few hours away
No, not really
Weetabix, you?"

And she tells me she had toast
And tea
And I think that sounds
Very grown-up
So I decide to try some tea
Tomorrow morning

At lunch Chloe sits on my bench with me
I read my sea life book
While she practices her magic tricks
I get to a page about the barreleye fish
Which is one of the scariest
So far

It lives deep down
And has eyes like telescopes
And a head
You can see
      Right through

I start to breathe
In a different
Pattern
In out in in in out in
And I can't
Fix
      It
No matter   how
      Hard
                     I'm

Trying

Then Chloe puts down her deck of cards
And slides closer to me

"You OK?"

I nod

"Are you sure?
Just
You're breathing weird?"

I want to run away
I want to run all the way home
And maybe
If I could catch my breath
I would
But I can't so I don't
So instead
I just tell her the truth

"I'm just
Scared"

She bites her lip
She's worried
I've made her worry

"But it's fine—"

"Of the book?"

She takes it from my hands
And looks at the page I'm on
Looks at the fish
And I imagine her laughing
Calling me a wimp
But instead
She slams it closed
And shivers dramatically

"Oh
Wow
No wonder you're scared
Why are you reading this?"

So I tell her
I want to know
Everything I can

"Even if it scares you?"

"Especially"
I say
"Because maybe
If I know enough about it
I won't be scared anymore"

She looks at the book
Thoughtfully
And opens it to the page about the barreleye

"You're so brave"
She says
Quietly
And even though I don't feel brave
Not in the slightest
Even though my breathing is still wonky
I decide to believe her
Just then
Just for a minute

"I'll trade you"
Chloe says

Like an old-timey merchant
Like I should prepare to barter

"Trade for what?"

"Information!"
She whispers it
Conspiratorially
And I feel
So suddenly
Like we're spies
On opposing missions
Working together
Against all the odds
And I stop focusing
So much
On my weird breathing

This
I've realized
Is one of the very best things
About Chloe

One minute
You're just sitting on a bench
In the cold
In a gray schoolyard
And then
You're a spy
Or a pirate
You're in space
Looking at Pluto
Or in the Amazon
Studying jaguars

With Chloe
You can go anywhere
Or be anything
In an instant
Without even leaving your favorite bench
Chloe has a whole world in her
And she's so good at sharing it

"OK"
I whisper back
Leaning in really close

"I'll tell you
A *highly classified*
Magicians-only secret
If you tell me
Something
About—"

                                        I hold my breath

"Fish!"

"Fish?"

"Yeah!"
 She's beaming

"Why?"

"Because"
 She says
"You know so much
You're always reading that book"

 I hold it to my chest

Suddenly and strangely protective
Defensive
Maybe
I feel very seen
All of a sudden

"And I just think it's so—"

    And
    I'm
    Holding
    My
    Breath
    Again

So what?
So weird?
So dorky?
So dumb?

"Cool"
She says
And when I look at her
She's blushing
Which makes my palms feel hot
And clammy

"I'll tell you everything I know"
I mutter

And she smiles

We decide to start the
Information trade
On Monday
So I have all weekend
To choose my very best facts

After school I spend all evening
In my book
Making notes about
The batfish
    Ogcocephalus darwini
    A fish with big red lips
    That crawls along the seafloor
    Because it can't swim so well
Until I'm sleepy
In a heavy way
Like my brain

Has reached its maximum capacity
It's all full up
On facts and feelings and thoughts and thoughts and
   thoughts

When Mum comes to say good night
I'm already
On the very edge of sleep
But I see her
Take in the mess on my desk
The paper storm
And do a little chuckle
Then she kisses me on the forehead
For five full seconds
And I'm asleep
Before she's even left the room

seven

Mum doesn't work Saturdays
So Saturdays are
Together days

We get up early
Not as early as schooldays

                                    Too early

But a nice kind of early
When the sun is still new and the sky is bright

We make pancakes
The thick kind

That fill you up straightaway
And make you feel warm in your middle
And we cover them with strawberries
And sticky syrup
And we drink hot chocolate
Usually

This time I ask for tea
And Mum looks at me
Funny
But she says OK
And takes my favorite mug from the cupboard
And when she hands me my tea
She kisses the top of my head
And that makes me feel warm in my middle
Too

Tea is weird
It tastes heavy
And grown-up
I add more and more milk
And two spoons of sugar
Only when Mum isn't looking

But by the end
I think I like it

After breakfast we do our chores
Mum does the dishes
I water the plants

                                    All three million
                                    My mum really likes plants

I fold all the dry clothes
And Mum puts our bedclothes in the wash

We open the windows
And let the cold air come in
And sweep over everything
Until it's all fresh and lovely and cool

Then we get our blankets
From the closet
And pour popcorn into the biggest bowls we have
And we burrow into blanket nests on the couch
And we watch a movie

This week it's Mum's turn to choose the movie
So it's black-and-white
And sounds a little
Fuzzy

Black-and-white movies
Make me feel
Sleepy
But
My mum
Loves them so
I try my very hardest to stay awake
As awake as a person can be

But I wake up somewhere near the end
To my mum
Crying
Just a bit
Quiet and private and important
And I don't
Know what
To do

I keep my eyes closed
Though that makes the word
Cowardly
Flash on my eyelids
In angry colors
Blood-red cowardly
Fire-orange cowardly
Deep, endless green cowardly
Ocean blue
Inky violet
Colorful cowardice
Is all I see and all I am
And Mum sniffles
And I try to tell myself
"Self
You are eleven
You are a child
It's OK
You are not a—"
But I can't listen
Because my mum is crying
And I'm right here
Leaving her all alone

I know that mums can cry
It's a thing that the smart part of my head knows
But that the squishy part
Refuses to know
To believe

I need my mum to be
OK
To be good and fine and
OK

Because I worry
About
So
So much
But I don't worry
About my mum
Because if I worried about my mum
If I let the Bad Thoughts
Stray toward her
I would shrivel
I would crumple
I would
Stop

I need my mum to be OK
Because I don't know enough yet
To save her
To fix her
To make her
OK
So I need her to be
OK
Until I know enough
Until I know it
All
Until I can protect her
Until I can keep her safe
Until I know
How

I keep my eyes squeezed shut
And Mum sniffles one more time
Lets out a big breath
And gets up
And pads out to the kitchen
All wrapped up in her fluffy bathrobe
And I stay
Very

Very
Still
And I try to stop
The flurry
Of thoughts
The mess in my head
The imaginings
The ideas
Every possible
Reason
Fighting for attention
All dashing around
Trying to find the weakest parts of me
The parts that will listen
She's crying because—
She's sad because—
She's scared because—
Because because because because
And parts of me
Believe them all

Mum knows that something
Is weird
Is off

But she doesn't know what
So she makes me a hot chocolate
And asks
If I want to watch another movie
My choice this time
She says she'll braid my hair how I like
And maybe we'll even make chili
(My favorite)
For dinner tonight

And I feel guilty
I feel guilty
Guilty
Guilty
I feel full up and heavy with it
So that my brain
Is spinning in circles
Trying to get away from it

We watch another movie
About spies and assassins
The funniest one I could think of
But nothing seems very funny
This time

Although Mum laughs
Big and loud

We do have chili for dinner
And we talk about how cold it's getting
And how I need a new coat
Because the sleeves are too short now
Or my arms are too long now
And we try to decide what to get my auntie Judith
For her birthday
In two weeks
And the whole time
I'm pretty sure
Only half of me is there
At the table
And the other half
Has separated
Has slipped out of me
And is floating around my mum like a ghost
Trying to find out what's wrong
Trying to find out how to make it
Better

I have a dream that night
That my mum
Is crying
She's crying and crying and crying
Downstairs
On the couch
And her tears are pooling on the floor
First a puddle
Then a pool
Then a lake
A sea
An ocean
Filling our house up like
An aquarium
The couch is floating
Bobbing against the ceiling
And Mum is still crying crying crying
And the water is spilling into every room
Banging doors open
Pushing against windows
Sweeping the furniture up

And I'm in my room
Standing at the door
And my toes are wet
And if I could just

Move

If I could just

Go

And my ankles are wet

And if I could just

Get to her

And

Comfort her

And tell her

It's OK

Then

I could stop this

Then

I could save us

Then

I could save her

But my calves are wet

My knees are wet

My thighs

My hips

My stomach

My arms

My chest

My shoulders

And I don't move

And I don't do

Anything
And it's all my fault

And then I wake up
And the water is gone
And the pressure ringing in my ears is gone
And I am dry and safe and warm
But the blame
Still squirms in my stomach

I can't get back to sleep
I try to read
I try to count sheep
I try staying very
Very still
But I can't sleep

I have pictures on my eyelids
Mum crying
Chloe falling
Me forgetting how to breathe
Clowns and
Zombies
And ocean and ocean and ocean

And my chest is starting to feel like
Someone's wrapped elastic bands around my middle
And I can't—

Dash dot dash dash
Dash dash dash
Dot dot dash

Dot dash
Dot dash dash
Dot dash
Dash dot dash
Dot

      You awake?

We learned Morse code
A few years ago
After my dad moved away

For the first few nights
I slept in Mum's bed

So we could keep each other
Company
So we could keep each other
Safe
So we could read together until sleep won us over
So I could wake her in the morning when she turned off
    her alarm
So she could wake me when I had nightmares

I had them most nights
Clowns at the foot of the bed
Red noses and wild eyes and big toothy grins
Zombies at the front door
Skin peeling away and bones sticking out
And me
Trapped

Mum got really good at knowing when they were happening
So she could wake me
Earlier every time
Until eventually
I barely even heard the clown start to laugh
Or the zombie groan
Just Mum

Saying
"OK
It's OK
You're OK"
Until my lungs remembered how to work right

Mum got good at waking me
And I got good at trusting her to wake me
And the clowns must've known
Because they stopped visiting so much
And then they just
Stopped
Altogether
And when they stopped
It was time to go back
To my own room
By myself

I didn't sleep at first
And I snuck back into Mum's bed
A couple of times
But she would wake

And trot me back in
And tuck me in
And check under the bed
And in the wardrobe
And turn off the light
And it would all just
Start over

After a week
We were exhausted
Both of us
So we went to the library
And we found a book
On Morse code
And we copied out the whole entire alphabet
On pieces of paper
That we stuck on the wall beside our beds

We were super slow
At first
And we got confused
A lot
But after a while
We were Morse code experts

Whizzes
We could send dots and dashes
Without even checking the paper on the wall
And after another while
We didn't even really need to anymore
Because we knew
We could
If we wanted to
And I could sleep
Again

Dash dot dash dash
Dot
Dot dot dot

        Yes

I reply
Knocks with my knuckle
Not too hard
Not too soft
Not too fast
Not too slow
Just the right length between letters

And I wait

But Mum doesn't send anything back
So I bite my tongue
And put my knuckle to the wall
And check the tatty paper on the wall
Just to make absolutely sure
I get it right

Dot dash
Dot dash dot
Dot

Dash dot dash dash
Dash dash dash
Dot dot dash

Dash dash dash
Dash dot dash

      Are you OK?

And then

Dot dot

Dot dot dot dot
Dot
Dot dash
Dot dash dot
Dash dot dot

Dash dot dash dash
Dash dash dash
Dot dot dash

Dash dot dash dot
Dot dash dot
Dash dot dash dash

      I heard you cry

I hear the springs of Mum's bed
Creak

Then the floorboards
Then her door
And then my light is switched on
And Mum is sitting on my bed
Looking confused and worried and sleepy

"When?"
She asks
Taking my hands

Today
I tell her
During the movie

And she looks down
And then
She lets out a little
Sigh
And I think she must be
Crying again
So I sit up
Ready to comfort her
To tell her it
Whatever it is
Will be OK
And that I'm here
With her
For her
But she isn't crying

"Stevie"
She looks into my eyes

In a way that I think means

This is the truth and you must listen to it

"Everything is

Completely

One hundred percent

Fine

I was crying

Because the movie

Was sad

Because it made me feel sad

And think of sad things

So I cried

And then

When I was done crying

I felt

Better

I felt OK again

Not all bad things

Are big bad things

Not all sad things

Are big sad things

Sometimes they just come and go

Just visitors

And we don't need to be

Afraid of them

OK?"

Oh
The relief is warm on my skin
And warmer in my chest
Which has been
Aching
All day
But now
Feels
Still
And
Calm

"Were you worried?"
Mum asks
And I don't need to answer
She knows already
"Stevie
You don't need to worry
About me
I'm OK
And if I'm ever not OK
It isn't your job to worry about it
Or to fix me
OK?
It's OK
It's all OK"

She looks at me
Really carefully
And she asks
"Do you worry
Like this
A lot?"
And I nod
And she says
"All the time?"
And I nod
And she nods
And her face transforms
Into her
Thinking face
Her answers face
And I feel
All of the worry
Fall off my shoulders
Because I can tell
My mum
Is on the case
And my mum
Is going to figure it all out
My mum
Is going to help me

And I hug her
Really tight around her middle
And I squeeze her so tight
That she makes a strangled noise and laughs
And I feel
Almost OK
If not for this one thing
Still sitting in my head
This one thing
Still in between me and Mum
My one secret
That I hadn't even realized was secret
And I let the words roll onto my tongue
Mum, I think maybe—
But before I can let them out—

"OK
Back to sleep"

So I just smile
And say OK
And tell her I love her
And decide
Maybe

That's enough fixing for one night anyway

And maybe

I can try again tomorrow

eight

On Sunday morning
I use the computer

It lives in the kitchen
And I can use it for homework
And looking up things
That Mum doesn't know
The answers to
If I ask first
So I ask
Can I please
And Mum says
Yes

And asks me
What I'm looking up today
And I say
Fish
Because it isn't a lie
Just only
Half the truth

Which doesn't
Really
Make it feel any better

So
I look up fish
First
Just to keep it
As true
As I can

I look up the
Odontodactylus scyllarus
Which is also called
The peacock mantis shrimp
(Thank goodness)

Peacock mantis shrimp
Are shrimp
That look
Like they've eaten
Rainbows

They're red and blue and green and yellow and they can punch
With the speed
Of a
Bullet

Mum plonks a mug of hot chocolate down beside me
Which makes me feel
Grateful and guilty
At the same time
And I think I might be
Allergic to secrets

What do crushes feel like?
I type it into the search bar

The squiggle in my chest getting
More wiggly and uncomfortable
With every word

A million results appear
Full of words like
"I just knew"
And pictures of boys and girls holding hands
Of Mickey and Minnie
And princes and princesses
Of cartoon girls with pink bows and long eyelashes
Blushing beside cartoon boys
With blue T-shirts

I sigh
None of this helps

So I start over
And with my shaky hands
I start to type
Can a girl
Have a crush on another—

"Stevie, can you—"

I jump
And smash my hands on the keyboard
Filling the search bar with
A mess of letters and numbers and symbols
And Mum appears behind me

I close the window
And stare at the fish on the screen
And Mum is still talking
But all my ears can hear
Is my blood
Pounding in my head

I'm going to have to try
Something else

I lie on the floor of my bedroom
All afternoon
With a notebook and my favorite pen
And I write
Everything

All of the feelings
All of the thoughts

All of the pictures that flood my head
When I see her
When I talk to her
When she smiles at me

I write it out
Then in a second of hot humiliation
I scratch it all out
And start over
And over and over
Until the words don't look so weird anymore
Until the words don't feel so strange

I feel warm
I feel like smiling
I feel
Aware of myself
Of all the good parts of me
Of how I'm smart and interesting and sometimes I'm funny
Because I think she sees those things
And if she sees those things then they must be true

I write it all
Again and again
Until I think
Maybe

I could say them out loud
Maybe
I could ask the question
What does it mean
Does it mean
What I think it does

By the time it's dark out
I've decided to ask my mum
Because mums know things
And I have a hole in my knowing
A big gap
Where there should be something
But there isn't
And I think it's a thing that matters
Because the gap feels
A little bit cold
And my heart feels confused and a little
Dizzy and fizzy and
Weird

"Mum"
I say
And she says
"Yes, Stevie?"
And I say

"You know Chloe
Who sits beside me
At school?"

And Mum nods

"Well"
I say
And I wish I'd planned better
Because words
Just come spilling from my mouth
And I have zero control
Over any of them

"She paints her nails"
I tell Mum
"Every week they're a new color
And by Friday
They're a mess
They're bitten and chipped

And I want to fix them
I want to paint her nails"

Mum looks confused
I'm not making any sense
None of my words are doing what I need them to do

"I want to touch her hair"
I blurt out
And Mum's eyebrows fly up
But I don't know what that means
And the not knowing
Makes it all worse
Way worse
Words are coming out fast
And I can't stop them

"I want to brush her hair
Because it looks soft
And I want to braid it
I think"

What am I saying
Why am I saying any of this

It makes no sense
It's all true
But it still makes no sense

"I like her more than anyone else"
I say
And the words stop
For a second
So I can take a breath
And wish wish wish for Mum to say something
But she doesn't
So I try

"It's like
How I always wanted that
Doll
The Barbie
Scientist Barbie
Because she was so pretty
And cool
And I—"

"Girls aren't dolls"
She says

And I know that
"Dolls aren't girls"
She says
And I know that too
And it seems that all she knows
Is stuff that I already know
So I zip my lips
And we watch TV

Usually when I ask my mum
Questions
Big or small or silly or smart
She gives me
Answers
Big or small or silly or smart

She wraps them up and hands them over
Like little presents
New things to know

And I unwrap them
And add them to my collection
And I feel
Better

But this time
I think she forgot
To put the words in
I think
She just gave me
Wrapping paper
With tape and ribbon and a bow
But nothing
Inside

And this time
I don't feel
Better
At all

I have a nightmare
That water is coming
And I'm standing
All alone
In the middle of a road
And I yell
But no one comes
They're all gone
And I think they must have known

So they ran

And they forgot me

Or they left

So I stand

Small and alone and me

And there it is

A wave

Stretching up up up

Scooping the clouds and pulling them

Down down down and

Crash

The wave hits

And water bursts over the whole of the world

And I hold my breath as I'm

Pushed and pulled and turned and twirled and I want to
  scream

But I know

If I do

The water will pour in

So I have no choice

I can be full of screams

Or full of water

So I swim

I swim swim swim

Up up up

Don't look around

Just swim up
And beg my breath to last
Until I reach the top
Until I reach
The surface
But I'm swimming
And I'm swimming
And I'm swimming
And there is no top
And there is no surface
Everything
Is water
And
I wake up
And I slap my hands to my mouth
And I cram my screams back into my mouth
And I swallow them
Down down
Down

nine

It snows all night
And when I wake up
The house is freezing
And Mum is on the phone
But she's put
Extra marshmallows
In my hot chocolate

I count them
Five extra mini marshmallows
And I wonder
If they're to make up for
The words she didn't give me
Yesterday

Five marshmallows
Five words
I suppose

I poke a half-melted pink one
With my spoon
What could it mean
Good or OK or fine or
Bad or weird or wrong
I don't know

Mum hangs up and sighs
And worry gurgles in my tummy
But she comes into the kitchen
Smiling
So I smile too
"Good news"
She says
And I look up at her
My brain already racing through ideas
Too fast to really see any
"You get a snow day!"
She says
And I can tell I'm supposed to be excited

So I smile big big big
And say
"No way!!!"
With extra exclamation marks
And she gives me a look
That can only mean
Love
So I really really look at her
And I blink extra hard
So my brain knows to please
Remember

Mum still has to go to work
Because
She says
Adults don't get snow days
Which seems very unfair

She calls my auntie Judith
Even though I insist I'll be fine on my own
And Judith says she'll come over at lunchtime
Which sounds fine to me
And terrible to my mum

Mum has me lock and unlock the door
Five times in a row
Just so she knows I know how

She teaches me how to use the microwave
Even though I've used it
A billion times

She shows me where the fire extinguisher is
Which is a little scary to think about
But I can see she's more scared than I am
So I roll my eyes
Like she's being silly
And pass her her gloves
And tell her to be careful in the snow
And tell her that I love her
And that Auntie Judith will be here soon
And that I'll be totally completely
One hundred percent fine and good and OK
And then she leaves

I watch Mum waddle to the car
A penguin on ice
And drive away
And I wave and wave and wave

Until she's gone
And then I find my schoolbag
And tip everything out onto my bed
And start looking for everything I need
For my expedition

Things I Might Need:

My notebook
Pens (blue and red and green and purple)
My water bottle
My mittens
My library books (all finished)
A flashlight (just in case)
The emergency cellphone Mum gives me for school trips
    and sleepovers
The bus timetable
My library card
My coin purse
Emergency ten-euro note from the bill jar

I need to know
What this feeling in my chest is
What it's called and
What it means and
Why it's there
I need to know
And when there's something
I need to know
I go to the
Library

So
I wrap up
Keeping to as many of Mum's rules as I can
Sweater
Coat
Scarf
Hat
Mittens
Chunky socks
And big boots

I check every power switch twice
And check the oven three times
Even though I don't think it's been turned on today at all

I lock
Unlock
And lock
Every door and window
Just to be sure

I don't like feeling
Anything but
Love
About my mum

It doesn't feel right

But right now
I feel
So many
Things
About my
Mum

I feel love
Always love
But underneath
I feel sad
And a little
Disappointed
I feel worried
And anxious
And mostly
I feel
Distant

Like someone grabbed us
Each of us
And pulled and pulled
Until there was a gap
Where there's never been a gap
Until there was
Distance
Where usually
We were
Together
Side by side

Like someone
Pulled us apart

And I'm afraid
I'm afraid
That that person
Was me

"OK"
I say
Sadly
To no one
In particular

To the walls
And the couch
And the TV
And the cactus on the coffee table

"OK"

And I open the front door

As I walk out the door
I grip the key

With its big fuzzy key ring
In a mittened hand
Right in front of my face
So it doesn't have any chance
To disappear

I walk carefully
I don't make eye contact with strangers
I look both ways before I cross the road
And go only when the little glowing person is green

I stick to as many rules
As I possibly can
So maybe
If Mum finds out about my
Fact-finding mission
She'll know
I never wanted to hurt her
Never ever never

ten

I memorized the bus timetable
When I was eight
Just in case
Mum always says
Just in case

So I know I need to walk
All the way to the bus stop
And wait for the bus with the glowy 32
And I know I need to pour exactly
€2.20 into the hole beside the driver

I feel the coins
Lots of little ten cents and twenty cents
And some little copper fives
They're heavy in my pocket
And I keep my hand
Buried in them
Just in case
They disappear

The walk takes twelve minutes
Which is five more minutes
Than usual
Because my feet kept sinking
Into the snow
And in my head
I imagine it is quicksand
And that I am in a jungle
Warm and full of monkeys
And lions and snakes
But then that gets
A little scary
So I stop
And come back to the snow and the cold

The bus arrives three minutes after
I get to the bus stop
And I'm the only one there
And there are only four other people inside
So I get the best seat
Right at the front

We speed through town
Through the snow and ice and sludge
And I count Santas
One two three
Four five six
Seven
And half a Santa poking out of a chimney

Seven-and-a-half Santas and nine minutes and the bus stops
And I am there

Our town's library is
Small on the outside
But giant on the inside

Because from the outside
It looks

Just like a normal building
Small and old
With red bricks
That are a little dirty
And super old
But on the inside
There are
Books
Books and books and books and
Books
Piles and stacks and shelves full and overflowing
And when you walk in
And you see all the books
And smell the paper and dust and warmth
You know
It can't possibly be small
It goes on forever
And ever

We haven't been to the library in a while
Just a little while
The flower beds are covered in snow
So the flowers must be sleeping
Under the ground

And the big tree
That looked like magic in the autumn
Is bare
But it still looks proud

I touch the trunk
And tell the tree it's doing
Just fine
And not to worry
Its leaves will come back

eleven

I'm not sure where to start
Which section would have the answer
To this
Particular
Question
I decide to start in the kids' section
Because that's the place
I know best

I feel safe there
Among the colorful spines
And covers with adventurous kids

There are squishy beanbags
And art on the walls
Of jungles and
Oceans and
Galaxies

And shelves and shelves and shelves
Of books
And I can read
Any one I want
I can read every single one
If that's what it takes

I start at A
And move through the alphabet
But by N
I still haven't found anything

I've found books about princesses and princes
About kings and queens and wizards and witches
About talking animals and flying cars and
Spaceships and aliens and whales and
Puppets and toys and bugs
But nothing

About a princess and a princess
Or a queen and a queen
Nothing at all
To answer
My question

I move to the history section
Which feels
Like the next safest place
Because this is Mum's section

My mum likes history books
Big ones
With pages thin as tissue
And words so small they look like ants
Running around
Telling stories
Of wars and expeditions and revolutions

Mum loves them
She vanishes into this section
Every time
Like an explorer
Or a time-traveler

Venturing into the past
And returning
With books that weigh more than I do
And an excited look on her face

The shelves are too high here
Me standing on my own shoulders
With another me standing on her shoulders
Still couldn't reach the top

So I start on the bottom shelves
And crawl along
Until I hit
China
Then Egypt
Then on and on
Around the world
Through decades
And centuries
And millennia
But still
Nothing

I plonk on the ground
In a corner
Somewhere between
The First World War
And the Second
Where no one can see me
And I pull my knees into my chest
And drop my head to my knees
And I try
Try try try my hardest
To breathe
In and out and in
And out

Coming here was a mistake
I know it now
Suddenly
Although I think I probably knew
All along
Or else
I wouldn't have lied to my mum

Good ideas don't need lies
I think

I feel lost
In a way I've never felt lost before

I know exactly where I am
And how I got here
And how to get home

But here I am
In a corner
Lost lost lost

Here I am
In a corner
Surrounded by all the information
All the answers I could ever want
Lost lost lost

And just as tears
Start to prickle my eyes
A voice
Says

"Oh
What's happened here?"

A surprised voice
A little stern

So I lift my head
And there
In front of me
Is the librarian

"The kids' books are over there"
She says
And I try to figure out how to tell her
No
This is where I need to be
But I'm not even sure about that anymore
So I just look up at her
And I must look lost or something
Because her face softens
And she crouches down beside me

I don't know why I didn't think of it before
If anyone would know
Where to find

A book
It would be her
It would be
The librarian
Of course
I start to feel
A little bit
Better

She has a friendly face
Round and soft
With laugh lines
That actually came from laughing
I'd bet

She has long brown hair
In a braid
With little wispy curls
Around her face
To me
She looks
Kind of a like a
Queen

Powerful and knowledgeable
How I want to be

She tells me her name is Susan
And asks
What I'm doing
Curled up in the history section
And she asks it
Like curling up in the history section
Is a totally normal thing to do
Like it isn't weird or surprising
At all

So I tell her the truth
Because I feel like I can

"I'm trying to find
 Some information"

"Well, you're in the right place"

She smiles and I smile too
Because it's that kind of a smile

She asks who I'm here with
And that's when the good feeling slips a bit
And I consider lying
I even get the lie ready
On my tongue
But it tastes
Bitter and wrong
So the truth comes out instead

"I'm here alone"

And she says
"OK
And does your mammy know you're here?"

And from the way she asks
I can tell that she already knows
So I shake my head
And she sighs
The expression on her face gets a little less soft

"Well,
Why don't you come up to my desk
And we'll see if we can find your information
And give her a call."

There's no question mark
And suddenly
I feel
Trapped

"No
Please!"

It explodes from my mouth
Not a shout
But too loud for a library
And people look at me
And Susan looks at me
And to my horror
My absolute
Horror

I start to cry

Susan puts a hand on my shoulder
And whispers
"Come on then"

And she guides me
Back to her desk

The librarian's desk
Is big
And wraps round
In a circle
Making a little round office
Like a spaceship
Right in the middle of the library
So when you sit there
Like I do now
You can see
Everything

I spin
Around and around and around

                                        Slowly
                        So I don't get dizzy and ill
                    So people don't look at me again

And I take it all in

And there are people
Lots of them
People I've never seen here before
Because usually
I'm at school
And usually
When I come here with Mum
It's full of other kids
In different school uniforms
All reading the new Wizards of Westerly Station book
And trying to guess the ending together
And yelling spells at each other
And being shushed

But today
It's full of old people reading newspapers
And looking things up on the computers
And mums
And dads
Reading quietly
To little kids
Little little
Like babies and toddlers and kids too small for school

There's a group of adults in a corner
Drinking tea and practicing English together
And two women chatting by the door
As they hang up posters about
Book clubs
And typing lessons

The library is full
And warm
And lovely
And I think
As I spin
That it's probably
My very favorite place

When Susan comes back
She hands me a big mug of tea
And a little sugar pot

"There you go"
She says
"That'll revive you"

I'm not sure what that means
But I like the sound of it

We sip in silence for a few minutes
Me still spinning
Slowly slowly slowly
In the librarian's chair
Her sitting on a stool she pulled over
Both of us watching people read and study and learn and
    chat

Eventually I say
"I'm sorry I was loud"
Because I am

And she looks at me and says
"That's OK"
In a voice that means
She's telling the truth
So I relax a bit
But in the same voice
She says
"You shouldn't go anywhere without asking your mum first
You know"

And shame floods my chest
I nod
Hard

"I know"
I tell her
"But
Well
I had to"

Susan shakes her head
And starts scrolling on the computer
Looking for Mum's number

After a minute she says
"Do you want to talk about it?"

"Talk about what?"
I ask
Although I already know
And she just gives me a look
Because she knows that I know

I sigh
And put my mug down
"Please don't call my mum

Not yet"
I cross my fingers
Under my chair
"I just need a little more time"

"What for?"
She asks

"Research"
I say

And she grins
Like I've said the exact right thing

"And what are you researching?"

And I open my mouth
To say
Fish
I am researching
Fish

But instead
My tongue
My teeth
My lips

Conspire against me
And my traitorous mouth
Blurts out

"Girls"

If she's surprised
She hides it well

Better than I do
I give my tongue a little
How-dare-you bite

"What about girls?"
She asks

And I'm not sure
How to
Answer

"Well—"
I start

"Not just
Girls"

She nods
Encouraging me to go on

"But girls
And girls"

I let out a big breath
Long and slow
A steady
Whoosh

"Girls and girls?"
She repeats
And I nod

"Girls and girls"

I tell her about Chloe
I tell her about her nail polish
And her magic tricks
And how she always has a banana at lunch

And writes the date in gold gel pen on her homework
And how I notice these things
And how I'm starting to think
I know why

"Do I have a crush?"
I ask
In my smallest voice
A voice so small
I didn't even know I had it
And I think I might cry again

"Or"
I ask
"Is there something wrong with me?"

Susan puts her tea down
Carefully

Then
She looks into my eyes
Straight into my eyes
Which are a little blurry
With tears I'm determined to keep in

And she says
"There is nothing
Absolutely nothing
Wrong with you"

And my tears escape
Enough for a lake
A sea
An ocean

I snuffle and snort a lot
I am not a tidy crier
I am a messy snotty crier
And I go through millions of tissues
I cry until I'm empty

But Susan just sits
And waits
And hands me tissue after tissue

With the first full breath I manage
I choke out

"Are you
Sure?"

And she
Does a little
Nod

And I laugh
And I don't know why
But I laugh
All the relief in my belly
Bubbles up
And turns to laughs
And I laugh
Until I have no laughs left

When I'm finished crying and laughing
And we've scooped all of my snotty tissues into the bin
We just sit

Susan looks sad and happy at the same time
And I'm not sure what I'm supposed to do with that

So I stay quiet
And add another spoon of sugar to my tea

"Have you tried talking to your mum about this?"

I tell her
"Yes
I tried
But I don't think I did it right
Because she didn't understand
And she usually does"

"And she never told you?
That it's OK?"
Susan asks
And her voice
Sounds heavier
Weighed down by something
Sad

"She did
I suppose
She told me

People could love people
That boys could love boys
And boys could love girls
And girls could love boys
And girls could love —"

But I suppose
She never told me
I could

"Silly"
I mutter

Why didn't I think I was part of
Everyone
How did I forget I was
Part of
Everyone

It all just seemed
Further away
Far from me
From my little life
In our little house
And my little classroom

"Am I dumb?"
I ask
"For not knowing
For having all the clues
And not putting them together?"

Susan shakes her head
She shakes her head
Fast and hard
Like the very idea
Is so
So far from true
That she needs to push it away

"I don't like feeling dumb"
I whisper really quietly
So no one else hears
I don't want to feel dumb or confused or weird anymore

After a minute
She takes a big breath
And says

"You read a lot,
Don't you?"

And I nod
Pride pulls my lips into a smile
So I take a sip to hide it

"Have you ever read a book about a little girl
Who is clever?"

I scan my memories
Then nod

"Do you remember how that made you feel?"

I blush a bit
And tell her
It made me feel clever
And it made me feel
Like it was OK
To feel that way
That maybe it was cool
To be clever
And a girl

Susan smiles
Mostly happy this time

"And have you ever read a book
About a kid who goes on a big adventure?
Who does something scary
Because it's important
Because it matters to them?"

And I nod again

"How did that make you feel?"

"Like I could do the same"
I say
"Like I could be brave
If I needed to be
Even if I'm scared
I could be
Brave"

"Then maybe we should find you some books
That can show you
All the other things you can be
Or feel
Maybe that might help?"

I nod
And it starts to make sense
Why I've been
So lost

I'm not dumb
Or silly
I just didn't have
All the clues
All the pieces
To the puzzle

Sure
I knew
People could love people
But those people
Were few
And far between
I guessed
Because I never
Saw them

I never saw
A girl hold a girl's hand

Or a boy kiss a boy's forehead
I never saw it

It's like the barreleye fish
With its see-through head
Or the peacock mantis shrimp
With its punch
Fast as a bullet
Octopuses with nine hearts
Sharks that cut circles in the bellies of fish

I know they exist
Deep inside
In the smart part of me
But I don't understand it
In the soft part of me
The feeling part

For that part
It's just too
Far away
And a little
Too scary

"Do you think that would help?"
Susan asks
And I nod
And she nods
And tells me that that's what we'll do then
We'll find books and
We'll find me in them

"I have to call your mum first"
Susan tells me
And I nod
And a spiky fear
Erupts
In my tummy
Like crystal in a cave
Jagged and cold

"What if—"
I start
But I don't know what the rest of the question is

What if
What

What if Mum is angry
Or sad
Or disappointed

It'll be my fault
All my fault

"I don't want to make my mum
Sad"

"She might be sad"
Susan says
"She might be
At first"

And I like how she says it
Like I can handle it

So I decide
Right then
To believe her
To be the kid

And let her be the
Grownup

I tell her Mum's number

When Susan hangs up the phone
She kneels down in front of me
And says
In a serious
You-must-listen
Voice

"Everything will be OK
And if it ever
Isn't
You know
You're safe
Here
And you are
Never
Alone
OK?"

And I say OK
And we go look at books

We pick out two books
I choose one about trains
And Susan picks out one
With two girls on the cover
Holding hands
And I hold it
And I stare at it
And it makes me feel
So many things
All at once
And for once
Every single thing I feel
Is good
And happy
And real
And true

Mum comes sprinting through the door
Twenty minutes later

She bursts in like she was thrown
Hectic and red-faced and covered in snow
Her scarf tangled in her hair

I watch her stop
And search
Looking for me
And I tell my feet to move
To walk to her
And tell her I'm OK
And not to worry
That I'm sorry
And I'll never do it again
But my feet
My feet won't go

Susan
Standing behind me
Clears her throat
And steps in front of me
"Don't worry"
She whispers
So so quietly
Only I can possibly hear

And she walks up to my mum
And says "Hi"
In her friendly librarian voice

"You're Stevie's mum, right?"
And Mum smiles and says yes and asks where I am and
    thanks her for calling
All so fast I don't think she took a single
Breath

She sounds
So scared
And of all the things I thought she would feel
All the things I thought
I would make her feel
Scared
Wasn't on the list
I never even
Considered
Fear
And I feel
Awful
For it

Guilt plops into my tummy
So heavy I feel like I might

Fall over
But instead
My feet start moving
And I run
Run run run
To my mum

"I'm sorry
I'm sorry
I'm sorry
Mum, I'm so sorry"
I chant
Like a song
But she doesn't hear
Because she's chanting
"Stevie
Stevie
Are you OK?
Stevie
Are you OK?"

I know she'll be mad soon
I know I'll be in trouble
For leaving the house
When I promised
Cross-my-heart promised

That I wouldn't
And I know that
But right now
All I care about
Is my mum
And how scared she sounds
And how scared I've been
Without even noticing
So I hug her
Tight tight tight

twelve

Susan helps us drag two big beanbags
All the way into the art section

I picked here
Because I don't think either of us
Have ever been here before
And it feels right
To go somewhere
New

Mum drops herself into her beanbag

And it makes a whoosh sound around her
She looks
Tired
Not sleepy
But tired
Like she's used up all of the energy
She had for the day
And now she's run out

I flop into my beanbag
Right beside her
And we look at each other
And I think
We both know
Just know
That something is about to change
The air feels different
Full of crackles
And my stomach feels different
Full of butterflies
Everything feels too sharp
I feel like I'm in a movie
Like aliens could walk in
Like I could sprout wings
Like the whole world might just   stop
And I wouldn't be surprised

I feel like there's electricity in my bones
And no part of me
Wants to stay still
I feel
Scared

Mum takes my hand

"Is this —"

She's looking at me
Really looking *at me*
And she looks
So like my mum
So like herself
Like I haven't really
Seen her
In weeks
Her face is so real and so clear and so hers
Her big green eyes
Just like mine
Her freckled nose
Her one dimple

She squeezes my hand
And the distance between us
The distance I was sure I felt
Evaporates
It's gone
So quickly
I'm not sure if it was ever actually there
Or if it was just me
Being
Afraid

So I look at her face
And it's the face that's there
When I wake up from my nightmares
That nods and smiles when I tell her what I learned at
    school
That laughs when I tell her jokes I make up
It's the face that I know best
So I look right at her
And I nod to say
It's OK
You can ask

And she nods back

"Is this about Chloe?"

And I think
She knows
She already knows
But I take a breath
Shaky but deep
And I tell her anyway
For me
And for her
I tell her

"Chloe has really nice eyes"
I say
Because in that minute it's all my brain offers up
"She has really
Really nice eyes

"And I'd never noticed
Anyone's eyes
Before

"I don't care
Really
If they're blue

Or green or
Brown or

"I don't care
I don't
Notice

"But I noticed
Chloe's eyes

"They're
Brown

"And they're really
Nice"

And I cross my fingers
In my pocket
And I beg the world
The whole entire world
Please
Let that be enough
Please
Let her understand

Let me be
Understood

And I open my eyes
And my mum is smiling a strange smile
And her eyes are wet
And she looks happy and sad and everything in between
And I didn't know a person could be
So many things at once
But here she is
A little shaky
A little worried
But still smiling

"I get it"
She says
"I get it"

And I cry again
And I've cried a lot today
But it's different
This time

thirteen

We're putting on our mittens
When the librarian's face
Lights up
And a little
"Oh!"
Pops out of her mouth and
She scurries off
Toward the history section
With a whisper-shout of
"Just a sec!"

She comes back a minute later
Red in the face

Carrying a book
It must have a million pages
And on the front
Are people
Hundreds of people
Cheering and chanting
As someone at the very front
Waves a rainbow flag
She hands it to my mum
And my mum's face does something funny
Like all her feelings want to be known
All at once
But then it smoothes out
And she just smiles
And says
"Perfect"
Really quiet
But she isn't looking at the book
She's looking right at me
So I smile too
Then we both hug Susan
And say we'll see her next Thursday
And she hugs back
And we go
Back out

Into the snow
Together this time

"So"
I say
And take a deep breath down to my toes
"I have a crush"
I swoosh the words out like a gust of wind
Fast fast fast
Full of all my breath and all my stress so now I'm empty
And my chest feels a little less tight
And my shoulders drop a little
And my body feels like my very own body again

"Yep"
Mum says
And she takes a breath too
Deep and wobbly
"You have a crush"
And we look at each other
And there's something in her eyes and I
Think I know
What it is and
Oh no

She explodes
In the loudest

"STEVIE AND CHLOE SITTING IN A TREE!"

"Mum, no!"

"K-I-S-S-I-N-G"

"Mum! No one even says that anymore!"

I blush so hard
The warmth melts me
Melts all of the bad feelings
All the fears and all the confusion
And the blush
And the warmth
Settle in my chest
So lovely and so sweet
A warmth so strong the ice around my feet might melt too

This feels
Like the very beginning
Like there's more to figure out
To talk about
To learn
But it doesn't feel so scary
Now
Because standing right beside me
Mum is giggling
Like I've never heard her giggle before
High and light and ringing
She's gripping her tummy
And laughing laughing laughing
And she looks
Happy
And she looks at me
Like I'm the very best
And I feel
The very best
So I laugh too
And we grip our sides
And we laugh
And laugh
And laugh
Until we can barely catch our breath anymore
And then

I scoop snow into my palm

And smush it between my mittens

And I chuck it

Right at Mum's head

And it hits with a splat

And she looks at me

Her eyes

Glowing

And we're still for a minute

Staring at each other

Red cheeks and teary eyes from giggling

And smiles as big as smiles can be

And then

Fast as lightning

She ducks

And then snow is coming right for me

And boom

It hits my chest and I fall

Flat on my back

And I snort

Because with my big puffy coat

And my mile-long scarf

I can't really get up
So Mum lies beside me
In the snow
Outside the library
And we make snow angels
And we look at the sky
The bluest blue I think I've ever seen
And everything
Everything
Everything
Everything
Feels
Just right

epilogue

In school the next day

When we're taking off our coats and scarves and gloves and
   hats

All of our armor against the snow

Chloe bounces up to me

With her hands behind her back

And pink on her cheeks

Maybe from the cold

But maybe not

I smile at her

Because now that I know

That what I feel is nice and good and

Normal
All I want to do
Is smile at Chloe

She smiles back
Bigger than usual
Like she has a secret
And no plans to keep it to herself

"Close your eyes and open your hands!"
"What?"
"Open your hands and close your eyes!"

I do as she says
And something soft touches my palms

"Open your eyes"

It's an octopus
A purple stuffed octopus
Eight tentacles tickling my palms
Big glassy eyes
Staring up at me

"I know you're kind of afraid
Of the sea

And all the weird fish and stuff"

For a second
I'm embarrassed
But only
For a second

"And I thought that this
Might help
His name is Sydney
And I'm almost sure
It's impossible
To be scared of him"

I haven't looked up at her yet
I'm just staring at the octopus in my hands
And trying to calm my heartbeat
Which is thumping along
So hard
I think it must be trying to tell me something
Heartbeat Morse code
I think
Probably
It's telling me to look up
So I do

And Chloe
Looks nervous
And proud
And happy
And something else too
Something
I think
I recognize
Something
I think
That I've been feeling too

So I smile
And I tell her
I love it
So, so much
I tell her it's my very favorite octopus
That I've ever
Ever seen
And I take
The deepest breath I've ever taken
And I think of Susan and the book she gave me
And my mum and all the teasing and chanting
And how it made me blush in the best
Warmest, most special way

And I let it fill me up with bravery
And I say

"Maybe, if it's OK with my mum
And yours
We could
Maybe
Go to the aquarium some time
And see them
For real?"

And the idea terrifies me
And lots of things terrify me
But today
Right now
In this moment
I feel so brave
I feel
So
Brave

the end